What is your favorite thing to do at a sleepover?

In the middle of the night, grabbing all the pillows and having an epic pillow fight!
— Tilli

Looking at the stars with a cup of hot chocolate, and a blanket on our knees.
— Ruby and Poppy

Telling each other scary stories!
— Matilda

Playing games and eating pink marshmallows.
— Roseanna

Making scary shadow puppets with your hands using a flashlight.
— Mischa

Sink your fangs into an Isadora Moon adventure!

Isadora Moon Goes to School

Isadora Moon Goes Camping

Isadora Moon Goes to the Ballet

Isadora Moon Has a Birthday

Isadora Moon Goes on a Field Trip

Isadora Moon Saves the Carnival

Isadora Moon Has a Sleepover

Coming Soon!

Isadora Moon Gets in Trouble

ISADORA MOON

Has a Sleepover

Harriet Muncaster

A STEPPING STONE BOOK™

Random House 🏠 New York

For vampires, fairies, and humans everywhere!
And for my wonderful parents.

Copyright © 2019 by Harriet Muncaster
Cover art copyright © 2019 by Harriet Muncaster

All rights reserved. Published in the United States by Random House Children's Books, a division of Penguin Random House LLC, New York. Originally published by Oxford University Press, Oxford, in 2019.

Random House and the colophon are registered trademarks and A Stepping Stone Book and the colophon are trademarks of Penguin Random House LLC.

Visit us on the Web!
rhcbooks.com

Educators and librarians, for a variety of teaching tools, visit us at RHTeachersLibrarians.com

Library of Congress Cataloging-in-Publication Data
Names: Muncaster, Harriet, author, illustrator.
Title: Isadora Moon has a sleepover / Harriet Muncaster.
Description: New York: Random House, [2020] | Series: Isadora moon; 7 |
Audience: Ages 6–9. | Summary: While at Zoe's house for a sleepover, half-fairy, half-vampire Isadora adds a little magic to the cake she and her friend are baking for the school competition.
Identifiers: LCCN 2019028913 | ISBN 978-0-593-12620-2 (trade paperback) |
ISBN 978-0-593-12621-9 (ebook)
Subjects: CYAC: Sleepovers—Fiction. | Baking—Fiction. | Contests—Fiction. |
Cheating—Fiction. | Magic—Fiction. | Fairies—Fiction. | Vampires—Fiction.
Classification: LCC PZ7.M92325 Iyd 2020 | DDC [Fic]—dc23

MANUFACTURED IN CHINA
10 9 8 7 6 5 4 3 2 1
First American Edition

This book has been officially leveled by using the F&P Text Level Gradient™ Leveling System.

Random House Children's Books supports the First Amendment and celebrates the right to read.

ISADORA MOON

Has a Sleepover

Chapter One

"We're going to have a competition!" Miss Cherry announced to the class one bright and flowery spring morning. "A *baking* competition! It's going to be like that show you all watch on TV: *Cake and Sprinkles.*"

"Ooh," said Oliver. "I love that show!"

"Me too," shouted Sashi excitedly. "I watch it every week."

"The winners," continued Miss Cherry, "will receive tickets to the season finale of the show. You'll get to be in the audience and watch it in real life!"

"Eeek!" squealed Zoe, next to me. The whole class started to chatter excitedly—

everyone except me. I didn't know anything about *Cake and Sprinkles.* I don't even have a TV at home.

My mom is a fairy, you see—she loves being out in nature and can't understand why humans like to "sit in front of boxes with moving pictures on them." And even if we did have a TV, I would only be able to watch

Cake and Sprinkles while Dad was out of the house. For him, it would be a horror show. He is a vampire and finds all food disgusting unless it is red.

"You will need to find a partner," said Miss Cherry. "And try to bake the most spectacular cake you can! The best cake will win the tickets. You have all weekend to make your cakes, and I will judge them on Monday morning."

"Eeek!" squealed Zoe again. "This is so exciting! Isadora, you'll be my partner, won't you?"

"Of course," I said, delighted. Zoe is my best friend not counting Pink Rabbit. He used to be my favorite stuffed toy, but my mom brought him to life with her wand.

"I've got a good idea," said Zoe. "Why don't you come to my house on Saturday? We can bake the cake and then have a sleepover. It will be so fun. We can sleep in the same room and tell ghost stories and have a secret midnight snack!"

"I would love that," I said. "I've never been to a sleepover before."

"I'll get my mom to ask your mom after school, then," said Zoe. "Oh, it will be SO fun. I can't wait!"

"We're going to have a sleepover too," said Oliver from behind us. "Bruno and I are going to make the best cake in the world."

"It's going to be a dinosaur one," said Bruno. "With green—"

"Shh!" said Oliver. "Don't tell them our plan."

"Oops, sorry," said Bruno, turning red. "It's not going to be a dinosaur cake."

"It's okay," said Zoe. "Don't worry—we won't steal your idea. We have a much better one!"

"We do?" I asked as we packed up our things to go home.

"Well," whispered Zoe, "not yet. But we WILL!"

★ ★ ★

"Isadora's going to a sleepover," Mom said at evening breakfast. We have two breakfasts in our house because Dad sleeps through the day and wakes up at night.

"A sleepover?" asked Dad. "Why?"

"For fun," said Mom. "Humans like them, apparently."

"They do," I said. "My friends are always having sleepovers. Zoe says you get to stay up all night and have a midnight snack!"

"Oh?" asked Dad, confused. "That just sounds like my normal life." He continued to suck his red juice through a straw, making a horrible slurping sound. When he finished, he wiped his mouth and said, "Humans are funny creatures."

★ ★ ★

The next day, I spent the afternoon packing my bag for the sleepover. I wanted to make sure that I didn't forget anything. I packed my pajamas with the bats on them, my slippers, my pillow, and my sleeping bag.

"That should be all of it," I said to Pink Rabbit. "Can you think of anything else?"

Pink Rabbit pointed at my wand, which was lying on my bedside table. I picked it up and put it in my bag.

"Good thinking!" I said. "It will be useful as a flashlight."

Chapter Two

By the time I had finished packing my bag, I was feeling a little nervous.

"Don't worry," said Mom. "I'm sure you'll have a lovely time."

"I'm sure I will," I said in a small voice. As we walked up the driveway to Zoe's front door, I suddenly wasn't sure if I wanted to go at all.

"Maybe I shouldn't stay the night," I said. "Maybe I should just go for a few hours, and then you can pick me up."

"If you like," said Mom. "But I think once you see Zoe, you'll change your mind. How about if I tell Dad to come and check on you tonight during his nightly fly? He can wait in Zoe's garden, and if you're still awake at midnight, you can look out the window and wave to him to show you're okay."

"Yeah, all right," I said, feeling a lot better. Mom knocked on the door, and we heard an excited pattering of footsteps coming toward it.

"Isadora!" shouted Zoe when the door opened. She jumped on top of me and gave me such a huge, squeezy hug that I dropped my bag on the floor.

15

"Hello, Isadora," said Zoe's mom, smiling. She looked so friendly and welcoming that suddenly I didn't feel nervous anymore. Mom kissed me goodbye, and I waved.

"Do you want to have some tea?" asked Zoe. "I've got my special dolls' tea set out. It's all ready!" She led me to the kitchen, where she had set the table.

"Mom let me make fairy bread, as a treat."

"Fairy bread?" I asked, wondering what it was. I had never heard of it, even though my mom is a fairy.

"Yes," said Zoe, sitting down on one of the chairs. "It's delicious. Look!"

On two small plates were slices of bread, buttered and covered in hundreds

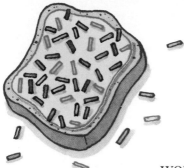

and thousands of sprinkles.

"I thought it would make you feel at home," said Zoe, biting into hers. I could hear the hundreds and thousands of sprinkles crunching between her teeth. "With you being half-fairy and everything!"

"Thanks, Zoe," I said, biting into my own piece of fairy bread. I didn't tell Zoe that this wasn't a real fairy thing. It must be something that humans had invented.

"It's yummy, isn't it?" said Zoe, crunching away.

I nodded politely. My mouth was too full of butter and cake sprinkles to speak. The fairy bread was nice, but not as nice as my usual peanut butter sandwich snack.

While we ate, we watched the small television on the kitchen wall. An episode of *Cake and Sprinkles* was on. Five people stood behind pale-pink counters, with mixing bowls and wooden spoons in their hands.

"Three, two, one, BAKE!" shouted the presenter, Whippy McFluff. She was so excited that her ice-cream swirl of hair was wobbling all over the place. The contestants quickly poured ingredients into their bowls. Butter, sugar, flour, chocolate chips . . . Both of us sat entranced, our eyes glued to the screen.

"Maybe we can get some inspiration for our cake," I said.

Whippy McFluff started to dance around the room, dipping her fingers into the contestants' bowls and tasting the different mixtures.

"Delicious!" she cried. "Ooh, zesty! Mmm . . . lemons." She beamed at the camera, all her white teeth flashing.

"She's so fun," said Zoe. "I would love to meet her."

"Well, maybe we can," I said. "If we win the competition."

Chapter
Three

When we had finished our tea, we went to find Zoe's mom.

"Can you help us with our cake now?" asked Zoe. "We want to make one that looks like it was made on *Cake and Sprinkles*!"

"Those cakes are huge," I said. "With five different layers—all different flavors. Coffee, chocolate, raspberry, lemon, and pumpkin!" I had never seen such wonderful cakes before.

Zoe's mom laughed. "You'll need a lot of ingredients for a cake like that," she said. "I'll have to go to the store if you're serious."

"We ARE serious," said Zoe. "We really want to win the tickets."

Zoe's mom looked at her watch. "All right," she said. "I'll head there now. We need some fish for dinner, anyway. Dad's in the backyard if you need anything."

"Oh, thank you," said Zoe, jumping up and down.

While we waited for Zoe's mom to come back, we went up to Zoe's bedroom. I love her bedroom because it is so interesting. She has butterflies painted on her walls and tons of posters stuck up on her closet door. She also has the biggest dress-up box of anyone I know.

"Can we play dress-up?" I said. I opened the box and began to look inside.

"Sure!" said Zoe, taking out some pink fairy wings and a sparkly silver crown. She put them on, then added a pair of slip-on shoes with pom-poms on the toes.

"I know," she said. "Why don't I be a fairy queen, and you be a vampire queen? We can be best friends, but the rulers of different kingdoms. My kingdom will be on a fluffy pink cloud! I'm going to have a palace there made from glass, and everything will smell like roses." She sprayed herself with a flower-scented perfume.

"Okay," I said, taking a tall, shimmery black crown out of the box and putting it on my head. "My kingdom will be up in the night sky, surrounded by glittering stars.

I will have one hundred pet bats. And Pink Rabbit will be a vampire prince!"

Pink Rabbit looked as though he liked my suggestion, and he began to hop up and down happily.

"Coco will be a fairy princess!" said Zoe, picking up her favorite toy monkey from her pillow and hugging it to her chest. Pink Rabbit watched with interest. Then he bounced over to Zoe and held out his paw.

"Pink Rabbit wants to shake Coco's hand," I said.

Zoe knelt down and held her monkey out to Pink Rabbit.

"Coco is pleased to meet you," she said, and Pink Rabbit's ears twitched with happiness. He began to stroke Coco's stripy tail.

"I think they like each other," I said.

"I think so too!" laughed Zoe. Then a wistful look came over her face.

"Isadora," she said. "Do you think that maybe . . . maybe you could bring Coco to life, just for our game? I think Pink Rabbit would love it. And I would too!"

I glanced over at my wand, poking out from my bag in the corner of the room.

"I guess I could," I replied. I ran over to my bag and pulled my wand out.

Zoe started to jump up and down with excitement.

"Could you?" she whispered breathlessly. "Really?"

"I'll try," I said. "I've only done this spell once before, though. It might take me a

28

few tries." I pointed my wand at Coco the monkey and squeezed my eyes shut. I waved my wand, then opened my eyes again. A stream of twinkly sparks floated down onto Coco, landing all over her fur.

"Ooh!" Zoe sighed in wonder.

The sparks began to fade, and underneath them Coco blinked her button eyes. The spell had worked on the first try!

Chapter Four

"Oh my," squealed Zoe, her hand flying to her mouth in astonishment. Coco twitched her arms and then her tail. Then she stood up shakily on her furry legs and jumped into Zoe's arms. Zoe hugged Coco tightly, and I could see tears shining in the corners of her eyes.

"Thank you," she whispered. "Thank you! Thank you!"

"You're welcome," I said. I was glad to make Zoe happy. Pink Rabbit was happy too. He was bouncing up and down by Zoe's feet, trying to get Coco's attention.

We began to play our game, pretending that Zoe's bed, with its pink comforter, was a fluffy pink cloud. We laid out a starry black cape from the dress-up box too. When I stood

on top of it, I was in my vampire kingdom, inside my dark, gothic castle with my one hundred pet bats flapping around me.

"I'm going to fly to your palace now," I said, and flapped into the air, flying the short distance across the floor and landing on Zoe's bed.

"I'm going to fly too," said Zoe, flapping her pretend fairy wings and jumping down onto the floor. She stretched both her arms out wide and ran around the room in circles. Coco skipped along behind her, and Pink Rabbit followed.

"I'm flying through the sky," she shouted. "It's full of fluffy pink clouds!" As I watched her, I had an idea. What a lovely surprise it would be for Zoe if I used magic to bring her pretend fairy wings to life!

When I was sure she wasn't looking, I waved my wand again. Sparks and glitter flew through the air, and suddenly her wings started to flap all on their own. Zoe began to rise up toward the ceiling.

"Oh my goodness," she squealed. "Look at me!"

"You're *really* flying!" I laughed, flapping my own wings and joining her in the air.

We flew around the room until we got tired and landed back down on the bed with a bounce. As we did, we heard the sound of a door opening downstairs.

"My mom must be back," said Zoe. She grabbed my hand, and we raced down the stairs together and into the kitchen, leaving Coco and Pink Rabbit to play in the bedroom.

"Gosh," said Zoe's mom. "You two look a little different from when I left!"

"I'm a fairy queen, and Isadora's a vampire queen," said Zoe.

"Well, if you two queens would like to wash your hands and put on some aprons," said Zoe's mom, "we can start making the cake!"

I felt a fizz of excitement as Zoe's mom started to lay out all the ingredients on the table: flour, butter, sugar, and eggs. There were little bottles of food coloring too, a slab of chocolate, and a piping bag for the frosting.

"It's like we're on *Cake and Sprinkles*!" said Zoe as she watched her mom measure out some sugar and butter and put them into two bowls. She gave one to Zoe and one to

me, and we began to mix the ingredients with wooden spoons. It was harder than I thought it would be, because the butter was still very solid from being in the fridge.

"We could use your wand to help it along a bit," whispered Zoe when her mom's back was turned.

"Oh, I don't know," I said, jamming my spoon into a lump of hard butter. "I'm not sure we should use my wand to make the cake. It might be cheating."

"Not really," said Zoe. "It's only to make the butter softer.

37

It will be just like using a food mixer! Our mixer is broken at the moment."

"I guess . . . ," I said. "Okay, I'll go and get it." I hurried out of the room and went back up to Zoe's bedroom.

Chapter
Five

Pink Rabbit and Coco were both sitting on the floor, looking at one of Zoe's books together. I grabbed my wand and ran back downstairs. As soon as Zoe's mom turned her back, I waved it over our mixing bowls. Sparks fizzed and twinkled, and suddenly

the butter and sugar in our bowls became perfectly smooth and mixed.

"YES!" said Zoe. "Perfect."

"Wow," said Zoe's mom when she turned back around. "Good job!"

She measured out some flour and poured it into our bowls. We mixed it in, together with some eggs.

"Now for the complicated part," said Zoe's mom. "If you want a five-layer cake, we need to split the mixture into five different bowls and then put a different flavor in each of them." She began to separate the mixture while Zoe and I watched. Then we helped her squeeze and zest a lemon for the first layer of the cake.

"This cake is going to be so delicious!" I said.

After the lemon, we added some raspberries to the second bowl of mixture, and then chocolate chips and cocoa powder to the third. I chose pumpkin for the fourth layer, and Zoe chose coffee for the fifth, even though she hates the smell.

"It's for Miss Cherry," she explained. "I know she loves coffee, because she always has a mug of it on her desk!"

Zoe's mom laughed. "That's a sneaky tactic," she said.

When the mixtures were ready, we poured them into five pans of different sizes. Then Zoe's mom popped them into her big double oven.

"We'll check on them in half an hour," she said, and left the room. Zoe and I peered through the oven doors at the five cake mixtures.

"You could do a little spell on them," said Zoe, "to make them rise really high!"

"Ooh," I said, a vision floating into my mind of a cake almost taller than us. I waved my wand, and we watched as the cake mixture in the oven began to puff upward, to twice the normal size.

"Wow," said Zoe's mom when she came in to check on the cakes. "Look how tall they are. Incredible!" She took them out of the oven and turned them out onto wire racks. They smelled delicious. While we waited for them to cool, Zoe's mom helped us make the frosting—a different color for every layer! Then she left us to frost the cakes.

"This cake is going to look amazing!" said Zoe as we began to spread the frosting onto the cooled cake. "We're going to win for sure!"

"I hope so," I said, opening a little bottle of sprinkles and shaking out tiny hearts and flowers onto the cake. Now that all the layers were stacked up, the cake was so tall that Zoe and I couldn't see over the top.

"What would make it look really spectacular," said Zoe, "is if the frosting was glittery. I've never seen glittery frosting before."

"Me either," I said, "but it's a great idea!" I waved my wand so that the frosting began to glitter. And then I waved my wand over the sprinkles too. They began to sparkle, crackle, and pop like tiny fireworks.

"AMAZING!" cried Zoe.

We continued to decorate the cake, adding some frosting here and a few more sprinkles there, and piping swirls and twirls all around the edges. I waved my wand again, casting a few more tiny little spells to add a bit more magic and flavor to our creation. When we had finished, we stood back and admired our handiwork.

"WOW," said Zoe, her eyes glittering in the reflection of our magical cake. "There's no way we won't win the competition!"

She began to dance around the room.

"We're going to win the tickets," she sang. "We're going to meet Whippy McFluff!"

I laughed, feeling really happy that Zoe was so excited.

"Oh my goodness," gasped Zoe's mom when she came into the kitchen a while later.

"What a fantastic cake!" She walked around it, admiring all the little details.

"I didn't realize I had bought glittery frosting," she said. "It didn't say so on the package. And look at those sprinkles— they're spinning around like miniature pinwheel fireworks. How clever!"

Zoe beamed, but I started to feel uncomfortable. Maybe we had gotten a little carried away with the wand waving.

Chapter Six

After dinner, Zoe and I ran upstairs to her bedroom. It was dark outside now, and time to get ready for bed.

"Let's lay out all your stuff," said Zoe excitedly. We opened my bag together and unrolled my sleeping bag.

"Do you have an air mattress?" asked Zoe. "Or should I ask my mom for one?"

"I've got one," I said. I dug around in my bag and took out a little velvet pouch.

"That's tiny!" said Zoe. "How can you fit a whole air mattress in there?"

"It's a fairy one," I said, opening the pouch and pulling out a small, fluffy pink cloud. As soon as it was out in the air, the cloud began to grow bigger and bigger until it was as big as a bed. Pink Rabbit and Coco immediately leapt onto it and began to jump up and down.

"Ooh," said Zoe. "It looks so comfy!"

"You can share it with me if you like," I said. "There's plenty of room!" Zoe pulled her comforter from her bed and laid it next to my sleeping bag, on top of the cloud.

"Oh, this is so exciting," she said. "I love sleepovers!" We both bounced up and down on the cloud with Pink Rabbit and Coco. Then we went into the bathroom to get ready for bed.

"Oh no," I said, suddenly remembering something. "I forgot my toothbrush!"

"Don't worry," said Zoe, opening a drawer underneath the sink. "We have a spare head."

"A spare head?" I asked. "What do you mean?"

Zoe handed me a big chunky toothbrush with a button on it.

"It's electric," she said. "I've put the spare head on it. Press the button!"

I pressed the button, and the toothbrush immediately began to vibrate furiously in my hand.

"Oh!" I said in surprise. I had never seen an electric toothbrush before. Dad would be very interested in this. I tried to squeeze some toothpaste onto the brush, but it was vibrating so fast that bits just kept whizzing right off it, splattering onto the walls.

"Hang on," said Zoe. She took the toothbrush from me and turned it off. "You have to put it in your mouth first, before you turn it on."

She squeezed some toothpaste onto the

brush, and I put it into my mouth and pressed the button. My whole head began to vibrate and my vision started to shake, but when I was done, my fangs had never felt so clean!

"I'll have to tell my dad about this," I said. "He's always interested in new hygiene products."

"Do you want to do a face mask?" asked Zoe, opening the drawer again and getting out two small packets. "I've seen my mom do them. I'm sure she won't mind." Zoe opened one of the little packets and took out a wet sheet of paper with three holes in it. It smelled like cucumbers. She put the sheet over her face so that only her eyes and mouth were peeking out of the holes.

"You look like a ghost!" I squealed, opening my own packet and putting the mask onto my face. It was cool and made my cheeks tingle. We both looked in the mirror.

"I don't know why grown-ups do these silly things," said Zoe. "We look so weird!"

"Maybe it's because they secretly like dressing up too," I said. "We look like monsters!" We began to dance around and put our hands up in the air like claws.

"Oooooh!" wailed Zoe. "I'm coming to get you!" She chased me out of the bathroom and back across the landing to her bedroom.

"What's going on up there?" called Zoe's mom from down below. "It's time to get into bed, girls!"

Zoe whipped the mask off her face and scrunched it up, and I did the same. By the time Zoe's mom came up to say good night, we were both lying quietly in bed, side by side. Pink Rabbit and Coco were snuggled between us.

Chapter Seven

"Good night, girls," Zoe's mom said, turning off the light and closing the door. "Sleep well!"

"Night, Mom," said Zoe.

We lay there in the dark for a while, although it wasn't really dark, because Zoe had a night-light plugged into the wall.

"We need to stay awake," she whispered,
"so that we can get up for a midnight snack!"

"Ooh yes," I said. "What are we going to
have?"

"Cake," suggested Zoe, giggling.

"We can't eat the cake!"

"I know—I was only joking. We'll have to find something else. Maybe we can eat the rest of the sprinkles. . . ."

"Maybe," I said, my mind drifting back to the cake. I was starting to feel a little bad. I kept thinking of Oliver and Bruno, and how excited they had been about their dinosaur cake. I knew they would have put a lot of hard work into it.

"Zoe," I whispered.

"What?"

"I don't think we should enter our cake in the competition."

"Why not?" said Zoe, sitting bolt upright

in the bed. "Of course we should enter our cake!"

"But we cheated," I said. "We used magic. I've been thinking about it all evening. I don't think it would be fair!"

"It was only a little magic," said Zoe in a quiet voice.

"It was more than a little," I said. "And really, we shouldn't have used any at all. We were having so much fun that we got carried away."

"But we HAVE to enter the cake," said Zoe again. "We want to meet Whippy McFluff, don't we?"

"Well, yes . . . ," I said. "I just—"

"Oh, I really want to win and meet Whippy McFluff," said Zoe, starting to sound upset.

"Okay," I sighed, not wanting to ruin the sleepover with an argument. I tried to change the subject instead.

"How are we going to keep ourselves awake?" I asked. "For the midnight snack."

"By telling ghost stories!" said Zoe, perking up again and giving a little shiver. She turned on her flashlight and put it under her chin.

"I'll start," she said, and she began to tell a story. It was about an old woman who walked the streets of our town after dark, dragging chains behind her that clinked and clanked all night long.

"That sounds kind of unrealistic," I said, thinking about the friendly ghost, Oscar, who lived in my attic at home. "Let me tell you about my real ghost!"

"But Oscar's not scary," said Zoe. "Ghost stories have to be scary. That's the point of them."

"Oh," I said, confused.

"Never mind," said Zoe. "Let's talk about our biggest wishes instead. Do you know what mine is?"

"To meet Whippy McFluff?"

"Close, but no," said Zoe. "My biggest wish is that we can stay best friends forever! And when we grow up, we can live in houses next door to each other."

"Oh, Zoe," I said. "That's a wonderful wish! I hope it comes true."

Zoe smiled and hugged Coco, who was snuggled up in her arms.

"What's yours?" she asked. "We need to keep talking so that we can stay awake until midnight."

"Hmm," I said, "let me think about it." The room went quiet for a moment, and all I could hear was the ticktock of the clock.

"I know," I said at last. "Besides staying your best friend forever, my biggest wish is to become a famous ballerina. A vampire-fairy ballerina!"

But Zoe didn't reply. She had closed her eyes and gone to sleep, tightly hugging Coco the monkey—who had fallen asleep too.

"I guess we won't be getting a midnight snack after all," I whispered to Pink Rabbit, and I closed my eyes as well.

But it was difficult to fall asleep. The little creaks and noises of the night sounded different in Zoe's house, and I wasn't used to

having a night-light in my bedroom. Also,
I was still feeling worried about the cake,
and about how we had cheated by using my
magic wand. The more I thought about it,
the guiltier I felt.

I was still awake, worrying, when Zoe's

glow-in-the-dark clock showed that it was midnight. Quietly, I slipped out of bed and walked over to the window. I looked out into the dark yard but couldn't see Dad. Maybe he had forgotten.

Then I looked into the sky and saw a black shape soaring toward the house, in the light of the fingernail moon. I opened the window as softly as possible and climbed out. Flapping my wings, I flew over to meet Dad in midair.

"Hey!" he said. "I thought you would be asleep by now."

"I couldn't sleep," I told him.

We flew up to the roof of the house

together and sat on the sloped shingles. Dad wrapped me in his cape, and we looked at the stars for a while.

"So tell me why you can't sleep," said Dad. "Is it because everything is different at Zoe's house?"

"Yeah, it is different," I said. "They have night-lights and electric toothbrushes, and a TV in the kitchen. But that's not why I can't sleep."

"Oh?" said Dad.

"We made our cake for the competition," I explained, "but we used my magic wand to make it look really incredible. And now . . . if we win, it will only be because we cheated. And it won't be fair to the others. I don't

know what to do, because Zoe really wants to enter the cake, but I don't think we should."

"I see your problem," said Dad. "But it's important to stand up for what you believe in. If you don't think it's right to take the cake into school, then you mustn't let Zoe push you into it. Even if she is your best friend and you want to make her happy. I'm sure she knows, deep down, that it would be wrong."

"Really?" I said, feeling loads better. "Do you think so?"

"I'm sure of it," said Dad. He smiled and ruffled my messy hair. "Now tell me a bit more about these electric toothbrushes!"

Chapter Eight

It was almost one o'clock in the morning when I flew back into Zoe's room and closed the window gently behind me. I slipped into the big, squashy cloud-bed and snuggled with Pink Rabbit. This time, I had no trouble getting to sleep. I closed my eyes, and the next time I opened them, it was morning, and sunlight was streaming through the window.

"Wakey wakey!" said Zoe, who was already up and bouncing around her room with Coco the monkey. She was busy getting out all her dolls' clothes and laying them on the floor.

"Which outfit do you want to wear, Coco?" she asked. "The striped dress or the romper?"

Coco leapt across the room and up onto the dresser. She did not want to wear any clothes!

It seemed like we waited a while before Zoe's mom called us down for breakfast. By the time we walked into the kitchen, my tummy was growling.

"My parents like to sleep in on the weekends," explained Zoe.

Breakfast at Zoe's was very different from how we have it in my house. We usually have toast and fairy-flower nectar yogurt, and red juice for Dad. But in Zoe's house it was bacon, eggs, mushrooms, tomatoes, sausages, and orange juice.

"Yum!" I said. As we ate, I stared at the

cake sitting on the counter behind the table. When we had finished our breakfast and cleared everything away, I touched Zoe's arm.

"We really can't enter the cake," I said. "It wouldn't be fair."

"But—" began Zoe, looking disappointed.

"It would be cheating," I said. "It would be awful if we won. Think about it."

"I suppose . . . ," said Zoe. She looked down at her hands and twisted them. "We won't enter it," she said. "But can we make another one before you go home? Without magic."

★ ★ ★

"Gosh!" said Zoe's mom when we asked her to help us. "Another cake? You must have really enjoyed making the first one."

"We did," I said, because it was true.

For the next few hours, we stayed in the kitchen and used up the rest of the ingredients from the day before. The second cake was much smaller and not nearly as impressive as the first one. But I felt much happier about entering it into the competition.

"I'll bring it in on Monday," said Zoe as I packed up my things to go home. She helped me squish the magic fairy-cloud back into its tiny pouch.

"I've had the best time," she said. "It's been the best sleepover ever!"

"It has!" I agreed, giving her a big hug. "Thank you for having me."

"Thank you for bringing my monkey to life," said Zoe, stroking Coco, who was sitting on her shoulder. "I know I only asked you to bring her to life for our game, but can she stay alive for always?"

"For always," I promised.

"I'll have to explain that to my parents somehow," said Zoe, and we both giggled.

Then I picked up my suitcase, and we went downstairs.

"Did you have a nice time?" asked Mom as we walked home together.

"The best!" I said, and I told her all about the two cakes we had made.

Chapter Nine

The next day at school, there was excited chatter in the classroom. My friends had all brought in their cakes and were lining them up on a big table at the back of the classroom.

"Goodness," Miss Cherry was saying. "I'm going to have trouble choosing the winner."

I scurried over to have a look at the cakes that had already been brought in. Sashi and Samantha had made one in the shape of a flower, with little butterflies perched on it. It was very pretty. Dominic and Jasper had made a cake shaped like a robot, covered in gray frosting, with gumdrops for buttons. In the middle of the table stood Bruno and Oliver's dinosaur cake. I could tell they had

put in more effort than anyone else had. Their stegosaurus cake was covered in green frosting, with triangle cookie spikes stuck all the way along its back.

They had modeled little trees and smaller dinosaurs out of icing and placed them around the stegosaurus to make an edible landscape. When I saw it, I felt more relieved than ever that Zoe was bringing the new cake and not the one full of magic. I wondered where she was. It was not like her to be late for school.

"Sorry, Miss Cherry!" came a voice from the doorway, and Zoe entered the room, carrying a huge cake. It was a towering, magical cake with glittery icing and tiny pinwheel fireworks spinning and sparkling all over it. A cake with five tall layers, each one a different flavor.

I stared at her and at the cake. My mouth fell open in horror, and I grabbed Pink Rabbit's paw.

"Wow!" said Miss Cherry, her eyes almost popping out of her head with amazement.

She hurried over to help Zoe lift the cake onto the table. It stood there like a mountain, looming above Bruno and Oliver's dinosaur creation.

"I'm sorry," whispered Zoe when she came to sit down next to me. "I just couldn't resist it this morning. I saw the two cakes sitting side by side on the counter, and this one just looked so much better!"

"But—" I said, starting to feel upset.

"Don't be mad," Zoe begged. She reached out for my hand under the desk, but I snatched it away. I felt like she had betrayed me.

"Isadora . . . ," Zoe whispered, her voice sounding a little wobbly now. "I'm sorry. I just—"

"Quiet, please!" said Miss Cherry, holding her hands up for silence in the classroom. "It's time to taste-test the cakes!" She went over to the table and cut a small slice out of each of them.

"Mmm," she said as she nibbled and chewed. "Delicious!" When she got to our cake, she took a tiny slice of each layer and tasted them all. Her eyes went big and round.

"My goodness!" she said. "These flavors are wonderful. The sprinkles are just POPPING in my mouth!"

"See?" whispered Zoe next to me, but she didn't sound so sure now.

"I declare Zoe and Isadora the winners!" said Miss Cherry, taking an envelope from her pocket and holding it up in the air. "The tickets are yours!"

Zoe stood up and walked over to the table. I followed her, my cheeks burning with shame. She took the tickets and held them in her hands.

"Your cake is a work of art," said Miss Cherry. "It must have taken you all weekend."

"It did," said Zoe, but her voice sounded

choked now. I looked across to where Bruno and Oliver were sitting. They were clapping along with the others, but I could see the disappointment in their faces.

"Well done, both of you!" said Miss Cherry, smiling. "Now, I think we'll all have a slice of cake." She began to cut the cakes up into little squares and put them on plates. As she did so, the class chattered.

"You can go and sit down now," Miss Cherry said to us, and Zoe started to walk back toward our desks, clutching the tickets in her hand. I followed her, still feeling angry and upset. I wondered if I should tell Miss Cherry that we had cheated.

Chapter Ten

Just as Zoe got back to her chair, she stopped and stood very still for a moment. Then she turned around and walked back to the table where Miss Cherry was cutting the cakes. I followed.

"Miss Cherry?" she whispered. "I need to tell you something."

"Yes?"

"Isadora and I don't deserve to win the tickets."

"What do you mean?" Miss Cherry stopped cutting a petal off Sashi and Samantha's flower cake and looked up.

"We, um . . . cheated," said Zoe in a small voice. "The cake wasn't all our own work. We used Isadora's wand to make some of it."

"Oh," said Miss Cherry. She sounded disappointed.

"I'm really sorry," said Zoe. "It was my fault. Isadora didn't want to enter the cake, but I brought it in anyway."

"I see," said Miss Cherry. "What a shame." She didn't seem cross, but she held her hand out for the tickets, and Zoe gave them back.

"I will have to judge again," she said.

"I know," said Zoe, staring down at the floor. I saw a little tear escape from her eye.

"Now," said Miss Cherry. "Sometimes we all do things we shouldn't. And you did the right thing in telling me the truth."

Zoe sniffed.

"And, winners or not, we can all enjoy some delicious cake now." She gave one of the plates to Zoe and one to me. We went

back to our desks and sat down. I reached out, squeezed Zoe's hand, and gave her a big beaming smile.

"Right!" said Miss Cherry. "There's been a change of plan. For reasons that I won't discuss, Zoe and Isadora have been disqualified from the competition. The new winners are . . . Bruno and Oliver!"

"YES!" shouted Bruno and Oliver, both leaping up from their chairs and dancing around the room. They looked so pleased

and delighted that I felt a glow of happiness warm my whole body.

"WOO-HOO!" shouted Oliver, waving the tickets in the air.

"It really is a most fabulous dinosaur cake," said Miss Cherry. "The best I've ever seen!"

Zoe looked down at her hands, and I knew she was feeling a bit sad about not winning the tickets and getting to meet Whippy McFluff.

"I'll tell you what," I said. "Why don't you come to my house next weekend for a sleepover? You can bring Coco, and we can make real magic fairy cakes with my mom. Then I'll get my dad to take us out for a vampire midnight snack on the roof of our house, and we can go flying among the stars!"

Zoe looked up, her eyes sparkling.

"I would love that!" she said, throwing her arms around my neck and giving me a huge, squishy hug. "There's nothing I'd like to do more."

Family Tree

My mom,
Countess Cordelia
Moon

Baby Honeyblossom

My dad,
Count Bartholomew
Moon

Me!
Isadora Moon

Pink Rabbit

Turn the page for
some fun things
to make and do,
inspired by
Isadora and Zoe's
sleepover!

Make a fang-tastic three-layer cake!

This cake might not be quite as big as Isadora and Zoe's cake, but it will still be spectacular!
Be sure to have a grown-up help you!

What you will need:

To prepare pan:
- butter, shortening, or cooking spray
- flour

For cake:
- 2 sticks butter, softened
- 1 cup superfine sugar
- 4 large eggs, lightly beaten
- 1-1/3 cups all-purpose flour, sifted
- 2-1/2 tsp. baking powder
- 1/4 tsp. salt
- 2 tbsp. cocoa powder
- 2 tsp. vanilla extract

What you will need:

For frosting:

- 2 sticks unsalted butter
- 4 cups confectioners' sugar
- 1 tbsp. whole milk
- 1 tsp. vanilla extract
- Optional: 3 drops pink food coloring

Method:

1. Preheat the oven to 350°F.

2. Grease three 8-inch round cake pans. Dust the base of each pan with flour.

3. Cream the butter and sugar together in a large bowl with an electric mixer until the mixture is pale and fluffy.

4. Slowly add the eggs, beating all the time. Then fold in the flour, baking powder, and salt.

5. Divide the mixture evenly among three bowls.

6. Mix the cocoa powder with 3 tablespoons of boiling water. Stir this into the batter in the first bowl.

7. Stir 1 teaspoon vanilla extract into the batter in the other two bowls.

8. Spoon the mixture from each bowl into a pan and bake for about 20 minutes, or until lightly golden. A toothpick inserted into the middle should come out clean.

9. Remove the pans from the oven and set aside for 5 minutes. Then remove the cakes from the pans and place onto wire racks to let them cool completely.

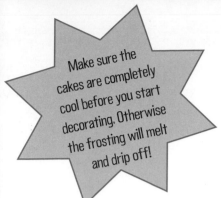

Make sure the cakes are completely cool before you start decorating. Otherwise the frosting will melt and drip off!

10. With an electric mixer, beat the butter for about 5 minutes, until it is light and creamy.

11. Slowly add the confectioners' sugar a spoonful at a time, continuing to beat.

12. Add in the milk, vanilla extract, and food coloring if desired, still beating all the time. The longer you beat the mixture, the lighter and airier your frosting will be.

13. Now you can start to build your cake! Spread the frosting on the tops of two of your layers. Stack the layers, ending with the unfrosted one.

14. Starting at the top, cover the whole cake with a coating of frosting. Chill the frosted cake in the fridge for 15 minutes to seal the crumbs.

15. Cover the whole cake with a second coating of frosting.

16. If desired, decorate it with sprinkles, sugar flowers, edible glitter, and anything else you can think of!

17. Chill the cake for another 30 minutes.

18. ENJOY!

Build a story!

At the sleepover, Isadora and Zoe try to stay
awake until midnight by telling ghost stories.
Play this fun game, for two people or more,
to make up your own stories! (They don't have
to be scary if you don't want them to be.)

1. Sit in a circle (or facing each other if
there are just two of you).

2. Choose someone to go first. That person
starts the story with "Once upon a time . . ."
and completes the sentence.

3. The next person must continue the
story, adding just one sentence.

This game is a great way to come up with some funny stories, and you can play as many times as you like. Write down your favorites so you don't forget them!

Which kind of cake are you?

Take the quiz to find out!

What is your favorite kind of cake?

A. I can't choose—they're all so tasty!

B. Yellow cake—it's good for carving into shapes.

C. Strawberry shortcake.

What do you think is the best cake size?

A. Gigantic! The bigger the better.

B. Middle-sized cakes are the best.

C. I prefer a small cake—it means I can eat it all!

What is the best cake topping?

A. Colorful sprinkles, swirly frosting, glitter,
and candles. And a bit more glitter.

B. My own creations made out of frosting and cookies.

C. A simple dusting of sugar.

RESULTS

Mostly As

You are Isadora and Zoe's sensational layer cake! You love to be the center of attention, and you think there's nothing better than sparkles and glitter!

Mostly Bs

You are Bruno and Oliver's dinosaur cake! You love being creative and making things with your hands.

Mostly Cs

You are Isadora and Zoe's second cake! You don't like to be too flashy, and you think simplicity, honesty, and tastiness are the most important things in life.

Sink your fangs into another
Isadora Moon adventure!

ISADORA MOON

Gets in Trouble

"This is George the iguana," said Bruno, holding out a large lizard-like creature for everyone to see. "He has a—a—*atishoo!*—a stripy tail and—*atishoo!*—he needs to be kept warm. . . ."

"Lovely," said Miss Cherry. "*Atishoo!*"

Bruno continued talking about his iguana, but he was finding it difficult. The air was becoming thick with stars and glitter. It wasn't long before everyone in the classroom was sneezing. Glitter can be very itchy when it gets up your nose!

"Oh dear!" said Miss Cherry through sneezes. "I think you had better go next, Isadora, and then maybe take the dragon outside for a bit."

I walked up to the front of the class. The dragon followed me excitedly, wagging his scaly tail.

"Um," I began, feeling a bit shy. "This is—*atishoo!*—a dragon!"

Every Isadora Moon adventure is totally unique!